FOMA THE TERRIBLE
A Russian Folktale

Translated by GUY DANIELS
Illustrations by IMERO GOBBATO

Foma the Terrible is one of Russia's "merry tales," a humorous story form which appears in no other literary culture. Guy Daniels' apt translation has been taken from a variant of *Foma Berennikov*, which Afanas'ev included in his famous collection of folktales.

The bumbling nearsighted peasant, Foma, inadvertently gains the admiration of two fine young champions, conquers the Chinese Emperor's grandest hero and his largest force of fighting men, and wins the hand of the Prussian princess—all as a matter of course.

wife live in Camden, Maine.

FOMA THE TERRIBLE

A RUSSIAN FOLKTALE

Translated by GUY DANIELS / Illustrations by IMERO GOBBATO

DELACORTE PRESS

To my niece,
KENT GIVENS

THERE once lived a squinty-eyed Russian peasant named Foma who was so big and powerful that if a sparrow brushed him with his wing he would fall flat on the ground.

One day Foma went out to do some plowing. But his old, skinny horse was too feeble to pull the plow. So Foma gave ùp, and sat down to brood.

Around a nearby manure pile, many flies were
buzzing. Foma picked up a dry branch and swatted away
at them with all his might. Then he began to count
how many he had killed. He got up to five hundred, and
there were still a great many left. Foma decided he had
killed more flies than anybody could count.

When he went back to where his old, skinny nag
was standing, he saw twelve big horseflies on her.
He swatted all twelve of them dead.

Then he went home to his mother. "Mamma," said he, "I have just killed a countless horde of ordinary ones, plus twelve mighty warriors. Plowing is not a fit job for a great hero like me; it's only for peasants. So give me your blessing, and I'll go out into the world to perform great feats of valor."

So his mother blessed him, wishing him success and great deeds on the field of heroic combat, and Foma got ready to go. Over his shoulder he slung a weed-chopping knife with a dull, rusty blade. Then he got on his feeble old nag and set off for his adventures.

He had been traveling along for some time, in a
strange part of the country, when he ran smack into a
milepost by the side of the road. "Aha!" thought he.
"This is just what I've been looking for! It's on
pillars like this that great heroes like me write their
challenges—in letters of silver or gold."

But he didn't have any silver or gold. So he reached in his pocket and took out a piece of chalk. Squinting hard, with his nose practically on the post, he wrote in gigantic letters:

THIS WAY PASSED THE GREAT CHAMPION,
FOMA THE TERRIBLE, WHO KILLED TWELVE
MIGHTY WARRIORS AT ONE BLOW,
AND FELLED COUNTLESS OTHERS BESIDES

Then he rode on.

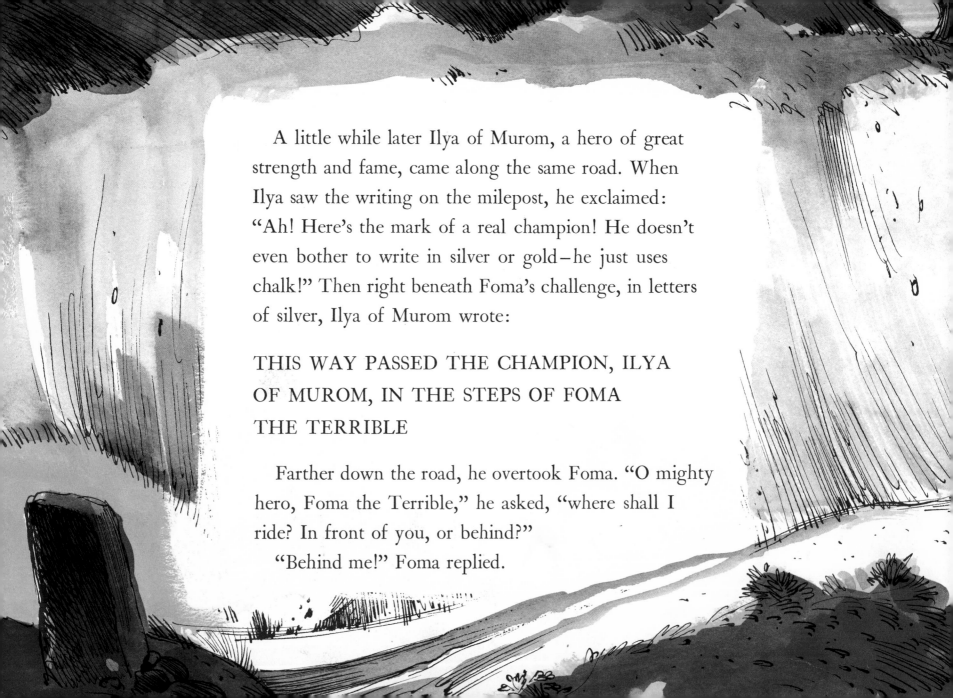

A little while later Ilya of Murom, a hero of great strength and fame, came along the same road. When Ilya saw the writing on the milepost, he exclaimed: "Ah! Here's the mark of a real champion! He doesn't even bother to write in silver or gold—he just uses chalk!" Then right beneath Foma's challenge, in letters of silver, Ilya of Murom wrote:

THIS WAY PASSED THE CHAMPION, ILYA OF MUROM, IN THE STEPS OF FOMA THE TERRIBLE

Farther down the road, he overtook Foma. "O mighty hero, Foma the Terrible," he asked, "where shall I ride? In front of you, or behind?"

"Behind me!" Foma replied.

Some time later another famed champion, young Alyosha Popovich, chanced to pass down the same road. When he saw the two inscriptions on the milepost, Alyosha Popovich felt his blood tingle. And beneath them, in letters of pure gold, he wrote:

YOUNG ALYOSHA POPOVICH PASSED THIS WAY IN THE STEPS OF ILYA OF MUROM AND FOMA THE TERRIBLE

When he overtook Ilya, some way down the road,
Alyosha Popovich asked: "Tell me, Ilya of Murom,
shall I ride in front or behind?"

"Don't ask me," replied Ilya. "Ask my big brother,
Foma the Terrible."

So Alyosha rode up to Foma and said, "O bold
warrior, Foma the Terrible! Tell me—where shall I ride?"

"Behind us!" Foma commanded.

In this way the three of them traveled a long distance, into a foreign land, until they came to a beautiful field. Here they stopped. Alyosha Popovich and Ilya of Murom put up their fine tents. Foma spread out his pants.

Now, this beautiful field belonged to the King of Prussia. And he, at that time, was at war with the Emperor of China, whose army was headed by six mighty champions. So the King of Prussia sent a message to Foma, saying: "The Emperor of China is making war against me. Can you lend me your help?"

Foma couldn't see very well. So he just glanced at the message, having no idea what it meant, nodded his head, and said, "Fine!"

When the Chinese Emperor's army got close to the Prussian King's city, Alyosha and Ilya came to Foma and said, "They are drawing near to the city, and to the King himself. He must be defended. Will you go yourself? Or do you mean to send us?"

"You go, Ilya," Foma commanded.

So Ilya of Murom went against the Chinese army and killed all six mighty champions.

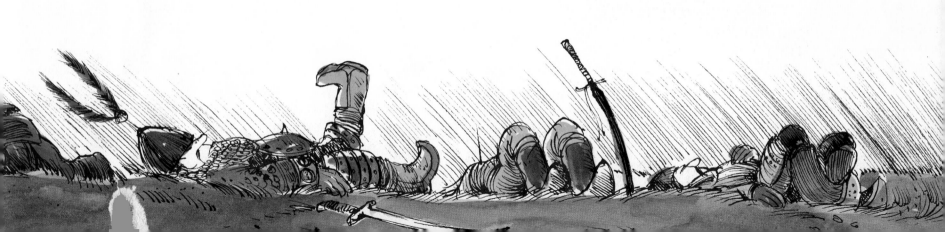

But the Chinese Emperor sent six more mighty heroes and a countless horde of troops besides. Once again Alyosha and Ilya went to Foma and asked, "Will you go yourself? Or do you mean to send us?"

"You go, Alyosha," Foma commanded.

So young Alyosha Popovich went against them. He killed all six mighty heroes, and all of the countless troops besides.

Then the Chinese Emperor said to himself, "I have only one champion left—the mightiest of them all. I've been saving him to sire others. But now I'll have to send him, too, into battle."

So saying, he sent for another whole army, and with it the great invincible champion. When the hero arrived, the Emperor told him, "It is not by his strength that the Russian warrior is defeating us, but by his cunning. But we'll outwit him. Whatever he does, *you do the same.*"

This time, as before, Alyosha and Ilya came to Foma and asked, "Will you go yourself? Or do you mean to send us?"

"I'll go myself," answered Foma. "Bring me my steed."

Alyosha's and Ilya's horses were roaming about, grazing in the rich green grass. But Foma's old nag was just standing there by the tents, gobbling up all of the oats.

This greatly vexed Ilya of Murom. He seized the old horse by the tail and threw her over the fence.

"I hope Foma the Terrible didn't see that!" exclaimed young Alyosha Popovich. "If he did, he will thrash us roundly!"

But all Ilya answered was, "See? The strength is not in the horse, but in the hero himself." Then he led the old mare up to Foma.

As Foma got into the saddle and surveyed the field of battle, he said to himself, "Now I'm done for! They'll kill me for sure! Well, so what? There's no shame in that." And off he went toward the enemy, scrunched down on his old nag's mane.

Toward him at a gallop came the Chinese champion.
Seeing Foma scrunched down, he remembered his
Emperor's command to do exactly the same as the
Russian, and he too scrunched down over the magnificent
mane of his gigantic steed.

Suddenly Foma pulled his old horse to a halt, got
down and began to sharpen his weed-chopping knife,
squinting his left eye as usual.

The Chinese hero was quick to imitate him. He stopped, got down off his huge charger, and started to sharpen his sword. When he saw that Foma's left eye was squinted, he thought to himself, "He has only one eye closed. I'll outwit him and close both eyes!"

The moment he did, Foma cut off his head. Then he seized the Chinese hero's great steed by the bridle, and tried to get on him. But he couldn't—the horse was too big. So he tied the huge beast to an oak tree, climbed up on a limb, and jumped into the saddle from there.

As soon as the mighty steed felt this strange rider
on his back, he snorted, reared back, and took off—tearing
the oak tree up from the earth, roots and all! Off
toward the enemy ranks he raced, with all his heroic
strength and speed, the oak tree streaming out behind
in the breeze.

"Help!" Foma cried out. "H-e-l-p! H-E-L-P!"
But of course the Chinese didn't understand Russian.

Thinking that Foma was letting out a war-whoop, they all panicked and started to flee. But the great steed bore down upon them, trampling them underfoot and flailing the oak tree about, smashing and killing every last one.

When he saw this, the Chinese Emperor sent a message to Foma, saying, "I will never do battle with you again."

That was all Foma needed to hear. Taking with him Alyosha and Ilya, who were still marveling at his great feat, he went to the Prussian King.

"What reward would you like?" the King asked him. "You can have all the gold you desire, or half of my beautiful kingdom, or else the hand of my daughter, the lovely Princess."

"I'll take the Princess," said Foma. "But make sure that the wedding guests include my two little brothers, Ilya of Murom and young Alyosha Popovich."

So Foma the Terrible married the lovely Princess.
And thus we see it is not only real heroes who triumph:
the louder a man blows his own horn, the better
he fares in this world.

A NOTE ON THE TEXT

FOMA THE TERRIBLE is a Russian folktale dating back to the seventeenth century—which makes it relatively young, considering that it has a Chinese cousin (a somewhat similar story) that goes back to the fifth century. The earliest known Russian variant was written down by one A. Zyryanov, a peasant of the Kurganskaya Oblast, and published in the mid-nineteenth century in the first edition of A. N. Afanasev's classic *Narodnye russkie skazki* (Russian Folk Tales) under the title of "*Foma Berennikov.*" Afanasev, whose collection is still regarded as the finest in the field of Russian folklore, later published a second variant; and numerous others have appeared since. But for sheer story-value, the earliest variant is still the best; and it is upon this Russian text that the present English version is based. The translation is rather free, with a phrase or word supplied here and there; but it is in no sense an adaptation or "imitation."

ABOUT THE TRANSLATOR

GUY DANIELS is an expert on the Russian language and is dedicated to translation as an art form. His works include adult books, poetry, literary criticism, and books for children, among which are *Timothy's Horse* and *The Falcon under the Hat*.

Born on a farm near Gilmore City, Iowa, Mr. Daniels is a graduate of Iowa University. He served in the Navy during World War II and since 1952 has been a full-time writer and translator. He lives in New York City.

ABOUT THE ILLUSTRATOR

IMERO GOBBATO was born and educated in Italy and has been a magazine illustrator, naval architect, movie set designer, and an art restorer. Mr. Gobbato and his wife live in Camden, Maine, where they enjoy being close to the sea.